428

b᷑   ..d Teachers

DK ᷑   ᷑ ..ing programme for
begi᷑   ᷑signed in conjunction with
leadin᷑   ᷑.

Beau᷑   and superb full-colour
photogr᷑   ith engaging, easy-to-read
stories to   proach to each subject in
the series   DER is guaranteed to
capture a   ᷑hile developing his or
her readin᷑   ᷑nowledge and love
of reading.

The five l᷑   ᷑RS are aimed at
different rea᷑   ᷑ou to choose
the books t᷑   ᷑r child:

Pre-level 1 – ᷑   ᷑ead
Level 1 – B ᷑n᷑   ᷑d
Level 2 – ᷑   ᷑nin᷑   ᷑ad alone
Level 3 – ᷑   ᷑ing alone
Level 4 – Proficient readers

The "normal" age at which a child
begins to read can be anywhere from
three to eight years old, so these levels
are only a general guideline.

No matter which level
you select, you can be
sure that you are
helping your child
learn to read, then
read to learn!

D0228039

LONDON, NEW YORK, MUNICH,
MELBOURNE, AND DELHI

Editor Kate Simkins
Designer Cathy Tincknell
Art Director Mark Richards
Publishing Manager Simon Beecroft
Category Publisher Alex Kirkham
Production Rochelle Talary
DTP Designer Lauren Egan

For Lucasfilm
Art Editor Iain R. Morris
Senior Editor Jonathan W. Rinzler
Continuity Supervisor Leland Chee

Reading Consultant
Cliff Moon, M.Ed.

First published in Great Britain in 2005 by
Dorling Kindersley Limited,
80 Strand, London WC2E 0RL
A Penguin Company

15 14 13 12 11 10 9

Page design copyright © 2005 Dorling Kindersley Limited
Copyright © 2005 Lucasfilm Ltd. and ™.
All rights reserved. Used under authorization.

020-SD173-Jun/2005

A CIP record for this book is available from
the British Library.

ISBN 978-1-4053-1000-0

Reproduced by Media Development and Printing Ltd., UK
Printed and bound in China by L. Rex Printing Co. Ltd.

Discover more at
www.dk.com

www.starwars.com

DK READERS

STAR WARS™
Journey Through
SPACE

Written by Ryder Windham

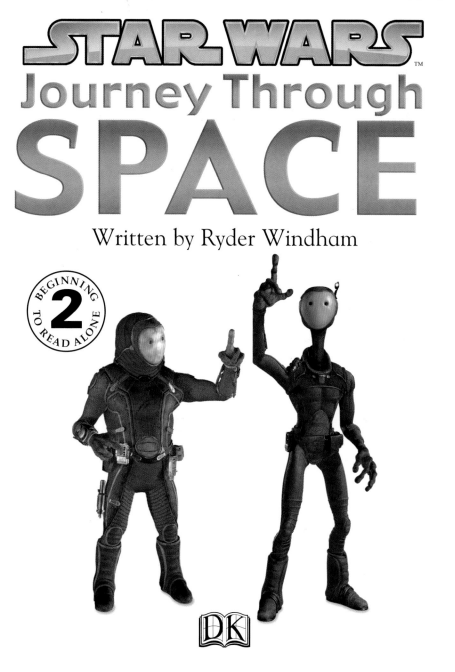

BEGINNING
2
TO READ ALONE

DK

Come on a journey through space
to the *Star Wars* galaxy.
It is far, far away.
In this galaxy, there are
many stars and planets.

Coruscant (CORE-RUS-SANT)
is the most important planet.
It is covered by one enormous city.
All the buildings in the city
are gleaming skyscrapers.

Jedi Knights
Many creatures live in
the *Star Wars* galaxy.
Coruscant is the home
of powerful warriors
called Jedi Knights.

Yoda

People and Gungans live on
the planet Naboo.
The people live in beautiful cities
on the land.
Young Padmé Amidala was once
Queen of Naboo.

*Queen
Amidala*

The Gungans live
in underwater cities.
They can walk
on land too,
although some are
a bit clumsy!
Jar Jar Binks
is a Gungan.

Jar Jar Binks

Podracing

Tatooine is famous
for Podracing.
In this dangerous sport,
fast vehicles race each
other through the desert.

The planet Tatooine (TA-TOO-EEN)
is covered by a dusty desert.
Two suns shine in the sky so
it is very hot.
Tatooine is a meeting place.
Space travellers visit the planet from
all over the galaxy.

Water flooded all the land on
the planet Kamino.
So the Kaminoans built their cities
on strong metal poles that stick up
above the water.

Kaminoans are very tall with long, thin necks. They ride winged beasts to fly and swim around their watery planet.

Geonosis (GEE-OH-NO-SIS) is not a good place to be captured. Prisoners are forced to fight huge monsters in special arenas.

Huge arenas
The arenas are made of rock. There are lots of seats inside.

Scary beasts are brought from other planets to the arenas.
The Geonosians look like insects and enjoy watching the fights.

Chewbacca

Tarfful

Kashyyyk (KASH-ICK) is a world
of giant trees and shallow lakes.
It is home to the Wookiees,
including Chewbacca and Tarfful.
Wookiees are tall and have lots
of shaggy fur.
They talk in grunts and roars.

Good friends

Chewbacca is friends
with a human
called Han Solo.
They fly together
in a starship – the
Millennium Falcon.

The planet Utapau
(OO-TA-POW)
has lots of deep holes.
The Utapauns dig
tunnels through
the rocks to join
the holes.

There are other
creatures on
the planet.

An Utapaun

Creatures called Utai (OO-TIE) live in holes in the ground.

Enormous varactyl (VA-RACK-TILL) wander around the rocky land. They are good climbers.

An Utai

The Utai ride the varactyl.

A varactyl

The red planet of Mustafar
(MUSS-TAH-FAR) is
a very hot place.
It is covered in fiery volcanoes.
Hot, melted rock called lava
flows from the volcanoes.
The sky is filled with black smoke
that blocks out the sun.

Fight on Mustafar

Two Jedi Knights,
Obi-Wan Kenobi
and Anakin
Skywalker, fought
each other
on Mustafar.
Anakin had turned
from good to evil.
Obi-Wan won
the fight.

The space rock known as
Polis Massa (POE-LISS-MASS-AH)
has a medical centre.
This is where space travellers can
go if they are sick.

The doctors are helped
by special robots
called droids.

Medical droid

Polis Massa doctors

Birth place

Padmé Amidala came to Polis Massa to give birth. She had twins.

The moon Yavin 4 is covered
in thick jungle.
The ruins of very old buildings
called temples rise above the trees.

At one time, the soldiers
who lived on Yavin 4 kept watch
for enemy starships from
the tops of the tallest temples.

What's inside the temples?

The temples were once used to keep starships. There were also rooms where people could eat and sleep.

The ice planet Hoth
is so cold that people can
freeze to death there.

On Hoth, people ride around on
large beasts called tauntauns.

Wampa ice creatures
live in ice caves.
They hang
the animals that
they catch from
the cave roof.

One time, a wampa even captured
a Jedi Knight!

The planet Dagobah (DAY-GO-BA)
is covered in thick forests and
swampy land.
The air is steamy, and it rains a lot.
There are many deadly creatures
and poisonous plants.

The Jedi Master Yoda went
to hide on Dagobah.
He lived in a small tree house.

Crash landing

Young pilot
Luke Skywalker
crashed his
starship on
Dagobah.
Yoda found Luke
and took him to
his tiny house.

Cloud City floats in the skies of the planet Bespin.

Visitors come to enjoy
its lively shops, restaurants
and hotels.

A cloud car

Cloud cars fly around the city.
They have room for two passengers.

The forest moon of
the planet Endor is
the home of small, furry
creatures called Ewoks.
They live in the trees and
use simple tools and spears.

At night, Ewoks stay in the villages that they build high up in the trees.

We hope that you have enjoyed your trip to the *Star Wars* galaxy. Come back soon!

Fascinating facts

There are millions and millions of planets and suns in the enormous *Star Wars* galaxy.

Some of the skyscrapers on Coruscant are more than a kilometre high.

The Queen of Naboo lives in the Royal Palace. This beautiful building has large windows and polished stone floors.

The trees on Kashyyyk are very tall. The Wookiees make houses in the trees.

The tauntauns have thick grey fur to protect them from the cold on Hoth.